Stone⬚

Writing and art b⬚

MW00764299

Editor's Note

And the flies were dancing and buzzing,
*   and joining in,*
and there was some sort of silent party with
*   no music,*
because the only sounds were the birds and
*   we wanted that.*
We never wanted it to stop, just wanted to stay,
*   my mother and father with their wine,*
laughing, me, running, slipping in the wet
*   grass, laughing at the chickens.*

In this excerpt from her magnificent poem
"On an Equestrian Farm [1]," Emma Hoff
perfectly expresses the feeling of being on
vacation (and especially a lazy July and August
kind of vacation!)—sitting outside, listening
to the flies and the birds, laughing, being
together, and never wanting it to end, while
also knowing it is so perfect and wonderful in
part because it will end. This summer, I hope
each of you enjoys at least one day that makes
you feel this way.

    And then consider writing about that day
or that week, turning to Emma's poems—
she has written two about her time on an
equestrian farm with her family—as examples.
In both, she captures the place and the way
she related it, masterfully mixing mundane
details with more philosophical observations.

Warmly,

On the cover:
Blooming (Acrylic)
Alyssa Wu, 13
Pleasanton, CA

Editor in Chief
Emma Wood

Director
William Rubel

Operations
Sophia Opitz

Design
Joe Ewart

Blog & Production
Caleb Berg

Customer Service
Tayleigh Greene

Refugee Project
Laura Moran

Stone Soup (ISSN 0094 579X) is published eleven
times per year—monthly, with a combined July/
August summer issue. Copyright © 2022 by the
Children's Art Foundation–Stone Soup Inc., a
501(c)(3) nonprofit organization located in Santa
Cruz, California. All rights reserved.

Thirty-five percent of our subscription price is
tax-deductible. Make a donation at Stonesoup.
com/donate, and support us by choosing
Children's Art Foundation as your Amazon Smile
charity.

To request the braille edition of *Stone Soup*
from the National Library of Congress, call
+1 800-424-8567. To request access to the audio
edition via the National Federation of the Blind's
NFB-NEWSLINE®, call +1 866-504-7300, or visit
Nfbnewsline.org.

StoneSoup
Contents

Rainy Day Colors (iPhone 6s)
Laylah Rose Burstein, 10
Berkeley, CA

Five Poems

By Analise Braddock, 10
Katonah, NY

Just One

No more than
one soul

Scattered the
Earth
Just one

No more than
one has
been found
On search
for more

Just one mind
Compared to
the nights'
thousand minds

Every light a soul
and a mind a
Bright
blooming
star

I don't have
more than
one

I don't have
more than
one mouth,
one mind,
one soul

Some have
many I see
They walk along

Talking
To themselves
And asking
In the reflection
Of the lake
"How do I look?"
They wait for an answer
"Perfect as always"
They walk with
Their many minds
And a thousand eyes
Holding a
Thousand souls
While I walk
With one
One soul
One mind
One heart
One set of eyes
One only
Just one.

Hands Open

I have held my hands open forever
I have let rain fill my hands with liquid
Glazing them with a beautiful scene
I have let life gift me with my soul
I hold pride by holding my hands out
I will hold them till all the green in the world is gone
And put in my waiting hands
Till the rain gives way and the
Storms retreat to a forever slumber
Till there is only me
Standing there
With my hands
Open
waiting

Eyes

I see the world
Has a path
Through the safety
Of my damp
Deep ditch

Overgrown with
The wild

Like a snake
Coiling around me

My body long gone
My eyes are intact

I see the
Sun blazing
High
I wonder

Could I ever reach
The sky?

I have no body I know
My clan and I
Settled in a ditch

With grass as
an itchy floor, ladybugs
All over

Counting their dots
So red so alive

I see the world
Through my ditch
So lively
So thrilling

What the World Is

The stars hold only one mind
The mind has a thousand eyes
The world will die down
Before the heart stops beating
For love
Clocks will wind and eventually stop ticking
Before hearts give out
The sky only has one world
The world has a thousand hearts
The stars

Secrets

I hear a secret, whispering to me.
The secret chooses me.
Only me, I am the only one.

Over the valley, past the frosty hilltops
Who knows this untold?
Though tempted to tell, not I.
I will keep this secret,

Till the end of the world
Till the animals go extinct
Till the sun is too hot for snow to hit the ground

I will keep my unrevealed
As far as the Earth is an ocean of trash
No green to be seen

In my heart it will stay
Stay till the world withers away
Forever you will stay.

In the Mist of Fog (iPhone 11)
Ohad Harosh, 8
New York, NY

The Squirrels, the Rabbits, and the Birds

Teresa observes the animal and plant life from the window of her home

By Teresa He, 11
Beijing, China

From the main window of our rented house in Wheaton, Illinois, we can clearly see the big tree by the sidewalk. It was a tree that stood sad and leafless in the winter, but we know that when summer comes around we will again see the tree shaking its neon-green leaves happily at us, as if in greeting.

Over the course of three years, we learned that the tree isn't only a beauty, but also a home. Sometimes I could see two squirrels on the tree's upper branches, hopping playfully. The tree is obviously where they live. It awed me to know that the big tree in front of our yard housed squirrels.

One time when we walked a nature trail, my mother picked up some acorns scattered all over the ground and put them in a bag. I knew what she had in mind. The next day, when we were walking out of the house, we saw that the acorns we placed on the ground the previous day were gone. A smile lit up my face as I imagined a squirrel lifting an acorn with its small hands, using its molars to nibble on it like a rabbit

would. They were truly adorable, these squirrels. They weren't always on the tree. Many times, we would see them doing their squirrel gallop across the sidewalk, sometimes suddenly stopping as if they had sensed danger, with their head cocked to one side.

The rabbits were other visitors. Seeing a rabbit in front of our house was rare, but it happened once or twice. Just below our main window there was a patch of soil that my mother used as her garden. She planted tulips there, but there was one area off to one side where tall, green grasses grew; she did not plant those.

One morning I looked out the window overlooking the small garden. Suddenly, a grey rabbit hopped out of the green grass. It was the cutest rabbit I had ever seen, and even plumper than usual. I wondered how it got so plump in the wild. I supposed it had made a home for itself in the tall grass, but that wouldn't be so enchanting because it meant the rabbit would turn to my mother's tulips as its main food. But I guess

Sprinkle of Dew (iPhone XR)
Miya Nambiar, 13
Los Angeles, CA

the grass was just a temporary home, because by the time I got back from school, it was gone. I kept wanting to see the rabbit in front of our house, but it never appeared again.

My mother hung a bird feeder from the roof of our house so that it was visible through the dining room window. We often viewed the birds eating while we ate our breakfast.

The visitors were mostly robins and sparrows, but an occasional northern cardinal also came to visit. Some birds would sit perched on the cable near the bird feeder, as if waiting for their turn. The sparrows were the pickiest ones. They would pick out the yummiest of the grains from the feeder, leaving little of those grains for the other birds. The birds only came in the morning, never at night. That's what I call an "early bird"!

The birdfeeder was handcrafted by my mother. She cut off two sides of a large plastic bottle and perched two chopsticks on the remaining two sides so the birds could stand. She filled the bottom of the bottle with bird food and hung it where we could see. It was simple, but its simplicity was its beauty.

These sights were shared with the squirrels, the rabbit, and the birds. Even though they are far away from me now, as I have returned to China, I need to remember them, so that is why I wrote it all down.

Growing

By Sophia Famolari, 9
Columbia, SC

A sprout is breaking
through the ground.
Adding beauty to
the world around.
A bright green plant
barely a stem.
Its stitching as
perfect as a dress's hem.
A closed bud, a
young bloom.
That will blossom
with colors better than
any room.
A beautiful flower
growing in the sun.
Now the growing is
all done.

A Road Through the Woods (iPhone 8, Lightleap)
Tatum Lovely, 12

Anita's Second World

Cory's feet are firmly planted on the ground—until she befriends her mysterious, fanciful neighbor

By Tatum Lovely, 12
Pipersville, PA

Once, underneath the beautiful London sky, there was a little back lane called Quinton Lane. The lane was made of cobblestone, and cherry trees lined the edges. Fog usually hung around. The fog seemed to say, "Ha! I'm not going anywhere. It's too much fun to make this lane and everyone in it all grumpy!" And it was true. The fog, and the frequent rain, and the dreariness and gloominess of spring just not coming, made the few houses of the lane seem to groan.

Though you could have made the argument that spring was already there, for it was mid-April. And the weather was rather warm. But the nights still grew very cold, making it impossible for a few small patches of snow to melt. Usually, the little children who lived on the lane loved snow! You could build snowmen, and have snowball fights, and catch snowflakes on your tongue! But this snow was not fun snow. It was not fresh snow, because it had not snowed in weeks. This was just dirty, leftover snow. Sometimes, the children would go out for hours trying to stomp away the last few piles. "Let spring come!" they would cry as they stomped. But

Quinton Lane remained dreary, wet, and foggy.

One old woman sat peacefully on a small bench by the side of the street, feeding the pigeons. She was glancing up at a window in one of the tall, gray houses. It was the nursery window, and in it you could just see the shape of a perfect little girl making up her bed.

Meet Cory Hanmay: Cory is what people would call a perfect little girl. She's polite, pretty, graceful, simple, amusing, and helpful. And does it all without getting her dress dirty. Now, she was making up her bed in her own beloved nursery. She was of the age of nine, but never wanted to go out and stomp on that dirty snow with the other children.

"Spring will come when it comes, and I'll leave it up to the cherry blossoms' own determined wills to decide when they want to bloom," she had said once. It was something that her grandmother had said, except not about cherry trees blooming, but about a runaway dog coming home. Cory was always quoting grownups— her grandmother, her mother and father, her aunt, and even the old pigeon woman. Cory was never being "childish and foolish", as she called it. She was too focused on becoming grown up and mature. She wanted to be the mother of five, when married. And she practiced constantly with her dolls.

When her bed was neatly made up, Cory went out onto her tiny balcony. The balcony had only enough room for one person and had strong metal bars, and was the same as every other house's nursery balcony on Quinton Lane. It was not quite raining, though it was certainly foggy, and leftover drops plopped down from the roof onto the balcony.

All the houses on the lane were almost identical and very close together. If Cory had a stick, she would have been able to reach out and poke the next house simply by leaning over the railing a little. The next house had a small window across from Cory's balcony. And Cory could not help but peering inside, for she saw a little girl around her age rummaging about.

She had seen this girl a few times before: on the street, in the park, talking mysteriously to the old pigeon woman, and now, looking into her window. Cory did not mean to spy—she really didn't. But it was only spying for a little while, for soon the other girl spotted her, and walked over to her window. She opened it and leaned out.

"Hello, Cory Hanmay!" she called.

"How do you know my name?" Cory asked.

"Are ya kidding? We're neighbors! I've seen you 'round," the girl replied.

"Well, I don't know your name," Cory replied.

The other girl thought for a moment. "I'm Princess Carolina of the North," she said proudly.

Cory examined her. She had long, jet-black hair and pale skin. Her eyes were a deep navy blue, and her eyelashes were the longest Cory had ever seen! And though the girl was rather pretty, Cory did not believe she was a princess.

"What's your real name?" Cory asked.

"Why, that is my real name! Well, in my Second World it is," the girl replied.

"Your Second World?" Cory questioned.

"Yes. My Second World. In it, I'm Princess Carolina of the North. And no, I'm not in the least embarrassed to admit that my Second World is . . . in my imagination. But in the imagination is the best place for something to be! Because there, you are always the queen, or king, or princess! Because you created it! So nothing can happen unless you happen it.

"Did you know? I live in a castle made of pink stone. It has thousands of windows and balconies, and very tall towers. And I have a garden of lollipops! There's a pond of melted chocolate, and the leaves on the many trees are edible! They taste like gummies."

Cory looked at her in awe, wide-eyed.

"But—but what's your name in . . . *this* world?" Cory asked.

"Oh. Well, I suppose you can know that my name is Anita Blakely," the girl—Anita—answered. "Now, want to go stomp on some snow?"

"Oh, no, thank you. I don't stomp on snow. I let it melt when it pleases."

"Aw! It's awful fun! How old are ya, anyway?" Anita said, pointing with her chin toward Cory.

"I'm nine. What about you?"

"Guess!" Anita demanded.

"Hmm . . . seven? I think you're seven or eight." Cory shrugged.

"Humph. No, I'm nine. Same as you. Why should I look any younger?" Anita demanded again.

Cory thought. Anita did not look too much younger. She was only a few inches shorter, and she had mature eyes. But there was something about the way she talked, the way she flicked her thick hair and twitched her pointy nose. And the way she acted spunky, and did not seem at all embarrassed to tell her about a completely made-up "Second World." This mysterious world actually interested Cory. It sounded delightful! She wanted a world like that. But it was only in Anita's imagination. Was the imagination really the best place for things to be? How many worlds could you have? Were you really royal in every one of them? Cory then realized that she didn't know much about imagining things. She was too busy focusing on reality. It would be foolish to imagine such things. They were fake. Cory dismissed the subject.

"I don't know. You asked me to guess how old you were. I did."

Anita giggled. Then Cory heard a woman from Anita's house shout up: "Anita! What're ya doing? Ya know

I got the bath ready! Your body isn't gonna clean itself!"

Anita rolled her eyes.

"Sorry, that's my nanny. She has been my nanny for, like, five years. She wears a green emerald brooch pinned up at her neck. It never matches any of her crazy outfits." Then Anita lowered her voice and whispered: "I'm starting to think she might be more of a ninny than a nanny." Anita chuckled carelessly.

"ANITA!" the nanny shouted again.

Anita sighed and yelled down: "Coming!" She smiled and waved at Cory, then disappeared inside the window.

Cory stared for a few moments after her, then slipped back into her own room, just in time to see her mother coming in with clean towels.

"Mother, what do you think of Anita Blakely?" Cory asked her absently.

"The Blakelys? Well, that's a question. They moved here a few months ago. They came from the United States. The father and mother always seem to be out of the house. Going here and there, though never together. The grandmother I've never seen. I assume she stays knitting inside. The nanny, well, I can't tell you much about her. She's plump, and likes to talk. But that's just what I've heard. Though I know nothing about Anita Blakely! Except I've seen her talking with the old pigeon woman. And she's their only child. They say the Blakelys . . . keep to themselves. And—no, I shouldn't repeat gossip.

Why are you so curious anyway?" her mother asked.

"Oh, no reason," Cory replied.

That same day, Cory's uncle, who worked at the nearby bank, called her into the living room where he was reading the paper.

"Yes, Uncle?" Cory asked.

"Jane tells me you were asking her about the Blakelys."

"Yes, Uncle," Cory replied. "Could you tell me anything more?"

"Nah, nah, nah. Well . . . maybe."

"What's that?" Cory asked.

"I just hear the rumors saying that the grandmother had been accused of witchcraft. There was no official trial, but some still have suspicions. Now run along. I can't tell you any more." Her uncle shooed her away and returned to his paper.

Michael, Cory's little brother, then came bursting in the front door, sulking.

"I ripped my kite! I was doing nothing but flying it high over the trees in the park, then the wind dropped and it just fell! Right into the trees. I tugged it down, but when I got it, it was ripped! Just like dat!"

Cory picked up the kite and examined the one small tear.

"Why, that can be patched up easily! I'll do it myself."

When the kite was fixed, Michael insisted on taking it to the park right away for a test flight. So Cory and Michael put on their hats and walked over to the nearby park. Cory thought it shouldn't really be called a park: it was just a large circle of grass with a small pavilion and two benches. But a park it was called, and a park it would be. Luckily, there was no snow in the park that day. Cory supposed that was thanks to the lots of children, enthusiasts of stomping on snow, who came to the park.

Then, while Michael's kite had taken flight, Cory noticed a girl sitting peacefully on a swing that hung from one of the trees surrounding the park. When she walked closer, she saw it was Anita Blakely. Cory began to turn back toward Michael, but Anita had already seen her.

"Cory Hanmay! Come over here!" Anita called, waving. Cory did not want to be rude, so she went over and sat down with Anita. It was not that she disliked Anita, but they were just so different!

"Hello," Cory said politely.

"Hey! I'm glad I saw you. I was just on a trip to my Second World. Queen Mara of the East was visiting, but our meeting can wait. When the Queen left, I was planning on making the trees dance."

"Making the trees dance? But that's impossible!" Cory said.

"In my Second World, only the impossible is possible," Anita whispered. While Cory was trying to make sense of that, she noticed a small pile of books next to Anita.

"What are you reading?" she asked.

"Oh, those? All sorts of things. Mystery novels mostly. Don't you just love books? Pages and pages of interesting facts or suspenseful stories on knights in shining armor! Authors fan the flames of our imaginations! Don't you think so?"

"Fan the flames of our imaginations? Uh ... yes. I suppose authors can do that."

A few days later, Cory was again standing out on her balcony, looking over at the open window on the next house. Again she told herself that she was not spying because she couldn't see anyone through the window. She just stared for a few minutes.

"Caught ya!" Anita called, leaping into view and making Cory jump and gasp.

"You were spying on me again. Why do you do it? I was in my Second World. Going on a journey. You see, I had to go visit the Island of Answers. I had to take a ship to get there. A great big ship, with many sails and a huge deck! The ship was called *Star Guided*. It was a long journey, but I liked it on *Star Guided*—the way the waves rocked you to sleep ... the salty, fishy smell that hung in the air ... the feeling of gazing out over the ocean .... It was magical."

Anita sighed, and shook herself out of her daze. Then a thick, heavy fog rolled in slowly.

Cory sighed loudly. "I knew that sunny weather would not last. It's always so foggy here on Quinton Lane. I hate fog."

"I don't." Anita shrugged. "I love fog. How it never really seems foggy right where you are, but all around you there is fog. How you never see it coming till it's all around you. How it rolls over everything like a warm blanket. I think fog is mysterious."

"Hmm. I think it's spooky. Like hundreds of ghosts floating all around you," Cory said.

"If you look at it that way ..." Anita smiled. "Well, I like ghosts too. The way they—"

"Please. You don't have to tell me all the reasons why ghosts might be fine. You won't change my mind," Cory said firmly.

"Fine." Anita laughed.

The next morning, very early in the morning, Cory was sound asleep, dreaming peacefully, when she felt something or someone violently shaking her. Cory murmured sleepily and rolled over. But the shaking did not stop. Slowly, Cory's eyes squinted open, and she sat up in bed. Her jaw dropped to see a little girl in a navy nightdress kneeling by her bed.

"Anita?! What are you doing in my room?"

"Shh! We must be very quiet. Now come on, let's go."

"What? Where are we going?" Cory asked, not stirring from under her quilt.

Anita looked around quickly to be sure no one was listening, then whispered: "We're going to my Second World!"

At this, Cory rubbed her eyes and stared wonderingly at Anita. "But I thought it was in your—"

"Hurry!" Anita urged.

This time, Cory did not hesitate. She obeyed and scrambled out of bed. Anita snatched up her hand and started pulling her toward the nursery door. Cory had time to get a quick glance at the clock, and groaned when she saw it was 4:36!

When the girls got to the hallway, Anita let go of Cory's hand and began tiptoeing down the stairs. Cory bit her lower lip and glanced back wearily at the nursery door. Finally, she took a breath and hurried down the stairs after Anita. They tiptoed past the study, and the kitchen, and the enormous grandfather clock in the hall. Slowly but unhesitatingly, Anita opened the big front door and slipped out into the chill of the fresh morning air. Cory slipped out behind her.

The breeze blew silently through her thin nightdress, and her bare feet felt strange on the cold cobblestone street. Again, Anita took her hand, and started running with her down Quinton Lane. It was a very foggy morning, and Cory could hardly see where Anita was taking her. They both nearly bumped into the large bench where the old pigeon woman usually sat. Once, Cory tripped and fell on a little stone on the street. Anita helped her up and they kept going. Cory's dirty-blonde hair blew behind her, whipping in the wind. Anita's hair was pulled tightly into two braids, whipping even more in the wind.

The girls dashed through the fog, Anita determined and Cory terrified. Cory's feet were nearly numb, and she dearly wished that she had put on her slippers. Finally, Anita stopped on the side of the street, next to a tall stone wall covered in vines.

"This is the place." Anita began knowingly brushing some vines aside while Cory sat on a large rock trying to warm her feet. She didn't know where they were, but didn't bother to ask. It was still dark, and the fog blotted out the stars.

Then Anita pulled Cory to her feet and motioned toward the stone wall where she had been clearing vines. Cory gasped. There in front of her on the wall was a brilliant silver door!

"How did—? But what—? Is that—?" Cory stammered.

"No time to explain. Come on!" Anita went to the door and slowly turned the huge silver handle. The door opened just a crack, and taking Cory's hand, the girls closed their eyes and held their breath and stepped through the magical door.

Cory opened her eyes and nearly fainted! It was exactly how Anita had described it. Through the door, it was no longer night. The sun peeked from behind the trees. A huge, pink-stone castle stood in the distance. And sure enough, a lollipop garden sat beside the pink-stone castle.

Cory then gasped again when she saw Anita. She was not wearing her navy nightdress anymore! Instead, it was a deep pink and blue dress, with elegant black stockings and shoes! She even had a little silver necklace and headband. Her hair was no longer in two messy braids but wrapped up in a large bun on her head.

But Cory was even more astonished when she looked down at her own clothes: she was not wearing her thin, white nightdress but a little pink dress with a sash and hoop skirt! She had white stockings and little lavender shoes. Her hair was now neatly combed and in two little pigtails on her shoulders. They were no longer cold, for inside the door it felt like summer.

"Where are we?" Cory asked, staring up at the pale blue sky full of puffy, golden clouds.

"Where are we?" Cory asked, staring up at the pale blue sky full of puffy, golden clouds.

"This is my Second World," Anita said proudly, stretching her arms toward the sky.

Cory did not speak. The view was too much to take in. She stood and stared out over the valley. She looked behind her, back to where they had come in the huge silver door. But the door wasn't there! Quinton Lane had disappeared, along with the cherry trees, and the park, and the fog, and the wall with all the vines—everything! Land stretched out all around them. They had entered Anita's Second World.

The girls began running down the valley and within minutes had arrived at the enormous castle. "And this," said Anita, panting violently but quite proudly, "is my castle!"

Cory, panting as well, looked up at the towering, pink-stone castle. "It's wonderful."

Anita stepped forward and pressed a large purple button. Cory heard a "ding-dong" sound inside the castle. A moment later, the large gate opened and a stout little figure appeared. The figure wore a bright cloak that covered his face. But a squeaky little voice sounded from underneath.

"Hello, ladies. Oh! Princess Carolina! You've come back! How lovely to see you again. And Miss Cory Hanmay! You look even more beautiful than our dear princess said you did. Please, do come in." Cory stepped inside and followed Anita and the stout little figure down a long entrance hall with many doors on either side. Then they came to the end and went through the biggest door of all, entering a large sunny room with an enormous throne in the center.

"Welcome to our dear princess's throne room!" the stout little figure said. Many more little people stood around the room in colorful clothes and cloaks.

"Cory, meet the Loolie Pops!" Anita smiled, motioning to all the little figures around the room.

Cory waved and looked around. The room was mostly empty, except for the large throne. The Loolie Pops came scurrying down to Anita and pulled her gayly up the small steps to the throne. Anita sat down gracefully and smiled down satisfactorily at her Loolie Pops and Cory. Then, the remaining little Loolie Pops rushed up to Cory, plunked her down into a soft chair, and began fanning her with little yellow fans that blew cool, fruity air gently toward her.

A little female Loolie Pop meekly came up to Anita and asked quietly, "Shouldn't we give dear Miss Cory a tour?"

"Wonderful idea!" Anita cried, throwing up her arms. Then the Loolie Pops began to chant and sing as they danced around the room.

"Oh, welcome to this delightful land! With our delightful princess! We'll show you the wondrous! Wonders! Of this wonderful land!"

Cory beamed, and Anita rose and

came to stand beside her.

"Why are we still here? Let's go!"

First Anita, and then the three Loolie Pops who chose to come along on the tour, showed her the lollipop garden. Then they went to the little forest with edible leaves on every tree. Then they climbed to the top of the tallest tower in the castle. Cory gazed wonderingly at the exceptional view. You could see far in every direction. Cory looked to her left and saw the forest and the lollipop garden. When she looked to her right, the valley went on for a while before a sparkling ocean began. The ocean went as far as Cory could see. It was so clear and glistening, Cory believed it looked like an ocean of fairies' sweet tears. And to make the view even more magical, a bright rainbow could just be spotted on the horizon.

"I wish we could chase that rainbow all the way to—wherever it leads," Cory mused.

"Who says ya can't?" Anita asked with a sly smile.

They dashed down the tower steps and emerged into the valley. They laughed and ran, spinning and giggling down to the golden shore. They halted on the small, shady beach and gazed at the beautiful sea.

"It looks even bigger standing here." Cory sighed.

Anita sat down on the sand and began pulling off her shoes and stockings.

"What are you doing?" Cory asked her.

"What does it look like? I'm seeing how the water feels." Anita pushed her shoes and stockings into a pile, then slowly waded out into the glassy water. Cory looked after her, then began taking off her shoes and stockings too. The water and wet sand felt good beneath her toes. The trim of her dress got a little wet, but Anita didn't care that hers was nearly soaked.

"We still gonna chase that rainbow?" she asked Cory, turning around to face her.

"How?" Cory asked. Anita took her hand and they both waded to shore.

"Come on. I'll show you." Anita and Cory snatched their shoes and stockings and started bounding down the beach. The three Loolie Pops skipped after them. As they turned a corner, a huge ship came into view. It was fairly far out in the ocean, for it would hit the bottom if it came any closer.

"Star Guided," Cory whispered, remembering Anita's story of the ship. Again Anita took her hand, and led her out onto a small dock. A little rowboat was tied to the dock, and Anita carelessly hopped in. Cory bit her lip, then looked out at that big rainbow.

"Cast off!" she cried, hopping in next to Anita. Anita untied the lines connecting the rowboat to the dock. Both girls picked up the oars and slowly rowed toward the ship.

When they got closer, they heard a man on the ship call: "Captain! The princess and the little girl are comin'!" Now many sailors ran to the side of the deck, and the rowboat came closer. When they were at the ship, the sailors cast down a rope ladder, and the girls carefully climbed up onto the deck.

"Welcome aboard Star Guided, me

girls!"

The sailors took care of the rowboat while Anita told the captain of their journey to the rainbow. The captain nodded and bellowed in a booming voice, "Raise the anchor! Lift the sails!" The sailors did as they were told, and soon they were off, sailing gallantly toward the horizon.

Slowly, the golden sun sank lower in the sky, and the clouds became a pale pink. Anita came to stand with Cory on the deck.

"Sunset over the ocean. Beautiful. So many colors—the purple and blue of the sky, the golden yellow of the sun and its light, and the deep misty blue of the sea."

"Yes," Cory mumbled. The sea breeze blew through their hair, and whiffs of that salty, fishy smell hung around.

"It's exactly how you described," Cory told Anita. Anita smiled and went below deck. Cory, with a sigh, soon followed her.

"Oh! Anita, I found more!"

Anita turned and ran through the tall grass to Cory, laughing. They had spent the night on *Star Guided* and now were on a large island searching for berries. When they awoke, the rainbow had disappeared. But then the girls had spotted the island and insisted on being dropped off.

"Ohh! You found red berries!" Anita exclaimed.

"And you're sure all the berries on this island are edible?"

"Positive."

The girls heard a rustling sound in the bushes nearby. They glanced at each other, then, mischief seeking, started stalking toward the rustling bush. Tiptoe, tiptoe, tiptoe . . .

"Boo!" A little girl leaped out of the bush and made Anita and Cory shriek. Cory was especially frightened. She looked at the girl, a little younger than her, perhaps. She had dark-brown hair in two pigtails that stuck out on either side of her head. Her dress was blue and red and all patched up. Her hands were scruffy, and she wore no shoes or stockings at all. Cory took a step back, but Anita leaped toward the girl, shrieking with laughter.

"Oh, Mildred! Didn't you give us the fright! Haven't seen ya in ages! About time I get to ask how ya been."

"Ha! Ya know I'm always doing fine. See ya got yourself some berries and an accomplice! Splendid. Hello, Cory Hanmay! Princess finally got ya to come 'round to her Second World, ey?"

"Yes. Did Anita tell you about me?" Cory asked uncomfortably. But Mildred did not answer. She and Anita had linked their arms around Cory and were skipping her through the grass.

"Yee! Wee! Hahah!" Mildred cried. When they finally stopped skipping, Cory brushed the twigs and grass off her dress indignantly.

"Hey, what do ya say 'bout eating some of them berries of yours?" Mildred asked spunkily. Anita found a big rock, and Mildred took off her apron and spread it over the rock as a tablecloth. Mildred and Anita sat down excitedly on the grass and dumped the berries out on the rock-table.

"Come over here, Cory!" Mildred called loudly. Cory sighed regretfully but came to sit on the ground around the big rock. The berries were very good, juicy and plump. When Mildred popped the last berry into her mouth, she sprang up and said flatly: "I should be goin'." Anita made no objections, but stood up and hugged Mildred goodbye. Mildred turned and waved to Cory, then skipped off, humming, into the tall grass. Anita slowly turned to Cory.

"So what did you think?"

"Oh, she's nice alright. Spunky, too. And—"

"No," Anita interrupted. "Not about Mildred—about my Second World!"

"Oh." Cory nodded. "It's wonderful. But we still have the whole journey back to the silver door!"

"No, we don't need the silver door. We can get back from here."

"Y-you mean we're done?" Cory whispered.

"Oh, there's lots more to show you, but another time. Come on, do as I do." Anita took Cory's hand and placed her feet a little apart. Cory did the same.

"I've had a delightful time," she told Anita as they both closed their eyes.

Anita smiled and squeezed Cory's hand.

"Don't open your eyes," she said.

Cory closed her eyes tightly and . . .

"Mmm . . . huh? Wha—?" When Cory opened her eyes again, she was lying in her own bed, in her own nursery room. Anita was nowhere to be seen. Cory glanced around. They were not in Anita's Second World anymore.

W-was it just a . . . dream? Cory thought desperately, climbing out of bed. It was now morning, and Cory pulled on her clothes and went downstairs. Her mother greeted her in the kitchen. She ate her oatmeal for breakfast. Michael asked her to take him to the park. Everything was normal. Nobody else seemed to realize how absent Cory was as she put on her shoes and went to the park with Michael.

"Oh! Look!" Michael exclaimed as they went outside. The cherry trees were blooming! The fog had vanished, and golden sunshine filled its place.

"Spring is here!" Cory cried. She and Michael rushed to the park where, to Cory's astonished delight, Anita sat quietly swinging on the little tree swing. Michael ran to play with his friends, and Cory rushed to Anita.

"Was it real?" she asked, sitting next to her.

"Was what real?"

"Your Second World! Which you took me to!"

"Cory Hanmay, I don't know what you're talking about. You know perfectly well that my Second World is in my imagination!"

"But—the silver door! And—and the dresses! Your castle! W-what about *Star Guided*? And Mildred!"

"And who on Earth would Mildred be? Cory Hanmay, I tell you that ya finally lost your mind."

Cory got up meekly. Disappointed,

she went back to Michael. It had all felt so real! But was it a good thing it had just been a dream?

Then the old pigeon woman, sitting quietly on her bench spreading seeds for the little birds, motioned for Cory to join her. Cory hesitated, but soon rushed over. She sat down with the old pigeon woman.

"So . . . how was your adventure in Anita's Second World, ey?"

"How did you—?!"

"I have some friends," the old pigeon woman replied, smiling slyly at Anita. Cory looked from Anita to the old pigeon woman. That was all the confidence she needed.

Four Poems

By Emma Hoff, 9
Bronx, NY

On a Painting by Henri Rousseau

In the savanna a tiger prowls,
but once tamed it can't ever regain its power.
It will sit behind the man,
whose eyes will be glued to his paper,
his blank paper with no writing,
because his hand does not move.

A child will stand there for eternity,
not growing,
eyeing the man and his tiger,
with a puppet,
which she wanted to bring to her special spot
that is taken forever,
her flower crown dangling in sadness,
unable to take another step.

If the hot sun beats down,
the motionless people will not feel it.
If its rays blind them,
they will be blinded like they already are.

The plants should grow or wilt, but they do neither.
They have decided on their size,
they have decided to be immortal,

to not move,
to not dangle,
to not fall.

If there is no wind, the hot-air balloons are not floating.
If there is wind, it is not real,
in an already unreal clear blue sky.
The animals?
They just stare,
and even that they don't do.

If you touched the lion it would not roar,
if you write something it will vanish,
if you take a step you're stuck.
Everything is frozen, yet moving.

Two Paintings

1. Girls under Trees (after August Macke)

Faces of the faceless.
What does she see now?
Blank and yet perfect.

Where does she go now?
Is there somewhere she can go?
Faces of the faceless.

The other girl,
what does she see?
Blank and yet perfect.

Does she have a face?
Or not?
Faces of the faceless.

Clutch that bag of grain!
It is also full yet clear.
Blank and yet perfect.

Just run, with your
eyes glued to darkness.
Faces of the faceless.
Blank and yet perfect.

2. Girl with Sheep (after Georg Schrimpf)

Rise above the ground,
head above the sky
giantess, hold your sheep.

Yes, lie down on your blanket of moss
and hold your miniature sheep and
rise above the ground.

Look into the baby's eyes,
he is not scared like the others.
Giantess, hold your sheep.

Your island,
floating toward the harbor.
Rise above the ground.

Last hope.
Last chance of joining.
Giantess, hold your sheep.

Let your river skirts flow.
Let your braid sing to the grass.
Rise above the ground,
giantess, hold your sheep.

On an Equestrian Farm [1]

Here I am.
Granting you the vision of the wooden chair
that we brought from the first living room
because we didn't have enough chairs for the dining room.
You see the fake flowers,
they will never live real lives, never die.
They will never smell like honey, never wilt.
They must always watch us,
the humans, do the tedious things we do.
The sliding door. With the bug screen.
Yesterday night we went through that door.
Out on the porch, we petted Trevor, who was not our cat.
We don't own the farm, we don't work on it.
We won't stay at the house. Soon, it will be all alone again.
And there will be no footsteps on the staircase.
And the painted china will no longer rattle
until the next people come.
And there is a little footstool
with its broken back. With a mahogany top.
Polished wood bottom. We do not get splinters on the floorboards.
They have been washed, sanded, many times. We see a little cart.
Also made of wood, oh pretty wood, and carved in ways that I couldn't
carve. I cannot carve.
The ladder in the back moves up and down,
the horse has run away,
tired of carrying your load of goods.
Outside, bright sun,
grass to run on, marsh where you can sink, sneakers and all.
The horses, they were angry,
or they just wanted to scream, neigh, someone, come!
And Trevor, ears perked up, hissed at a bird that was too loud,
too happy.
And yet, Trevor did not move from his place on the porch.

He just glared like a madman and settled down, ready to be petted
some more. And my mother lounged in a chair,
and my father had gone inside with his camera, only to come out again.
And the flies were dancing and buzzing, and joining in,
and there was some sort of silent party with no music,
because the only sounds were the birds and we wanted that.
We never wanted it to stop, just wanted to stay, my mother and father with
their wine, laughing, me, running, slipping in the wet grass, laughing at the
        chickens.
The chicken that came up the steps with its loud claws,
the chicken that greeted me with the call of its throat,
the chicken I shied from,
the chicken with menacing eyes,
and yet Trevor's yellow eyes were more menacing.
And the barn held nothing but chickens and horses,
and the occasional cat, of which there were three.
Two cats would not greet us, were not friendly.
One ran into the bushes, another stayed on the porch, back arched.
The calico, and the tuxedo.
We don't have names for those yet.
They are not ours, do not want to be ours.
We have no ocean in front of our house, yet all of the paintings on
the walls are farms, farms with oceans stretching, waking from deep
        sleeps.
Our house, the house that is not really ours, has a dirt road in front of it.
No, gravel. We have no forest either.
No boat approaching the forest.
Why do the paintings lie?
Are these real places, or are they just what someone wants to see?
One of the chairs has vines engulfing it,
yet the vines are just patterns. You cannot feel them. They are not real.
There are many doors
in the house. And so many closets, with locks that are rusted shut.
One closet opened and had a light with a chain so you could turn it on,
and a staircase, which led to a ceiling on which you could bump

your head. There is nothing to walk towards.
And there is a rug in the second living room,
which has pretty flower patterns on it,
on which you can roll and become the flowers.
These flowers aren't trying hard, don't have bright pink colors.
These flowers are brown, perfect.

The Old Water Wheel (Samsung Galaxy S8)
Lucas Hinds, 13
Lenoir City, TN

On an Equestrian Farm [2]

There was a day on the farm that was not like the others.

Because the orange cat (we named her Claire) had finally come up to us,

and she was ready to flirt with us. She meowed at us, begged us for attention with

mischievous eyes, but when we tried to pet her,

oh, the sight! She scurried away as if we were hurting her.

She told us she thought our hands were dirty, and if we were a self-conscious
family

we would have looked at our hands,

and we would have run inside and washed them and glared at the cat out the
window,

who would be licking herself like nothing had happened.

This was the day that we learned a funny thing, that Trevor was a girl

and that Claire and the black-and-white cat (Patricia, Pat for short)

were boys, through and through. And yet, as we learned their real names, we

forgot them all the same, and the only cat's name we could remember was
Trevor's.

Trevor's name was Fern, and my parents called her that,

but I was so used to Trevor that I continued to mix up the cats,

girl for boy, boy for girl.

And then we met another miracle! A miracle that only nature herself could have
given us.

Another cat, who did not belong to the people on the farm

but came and ate all the food anyway.

And this cat's name was a name that I remembered:

Lint. Like the stuff that sticks to clothes. This cat stuck to the farm,

with its grassy hills and beautiful skies, and the high grass that my dad led my

mom and me into, despite my warnings of tick territory

(it did turn out to be tick territory),

and so we squelched through mud, only to find that the forest did not have a trail,

as my dad had hoped, so we squelched back to the house,

and we took showers and glared at my dad. And onwards our adventures

stretched throughout the week we stayed, so many I cannot tell you about all of

them, and they were too perfect and beautiful to be written down in words
anyway,

and it will exhaust me to tell the tale out loud,
so I am content the way things are. I know nobody likes cliffhangers.
But hold onto the cliff and climb up onto it
and you will see the farm, and everything we did there.

The Failing Night

After a fight with her dad, the narrator decides to run away

By Lindsay Gale, 9
Dublin, Ohio

My fists were still clenched. Anger coursed through my veins like acidic fire. Just minutes ago, my dad and I had been arguing about a math problem I didn't know how to do. I gritted my teeth just thinking about it. I had realized the answer after a lot of yelling and arguing. Then, red-faced, Dad had ordered me to go to my room.

The anger was a burning pit of rage in my chest. I realized how unfair this was. I had to stop it. I hated all of these rules. They held me back, confining me in restraints much stronger than typical chains. Just this one time my parents had treated me horribly made me think of all the other times. They were like bars striking at me, cold and unforgiving. My rage fired up, threatening to overtake my thoughts. I looked around, trying to calm myself.

Then my eyes landed on my bookshelf, where *Hatchet, The Evolution of Calpurnia Tate, Caddie Woodlawn,* and a bunch of survival guides were displayed proudly. I love the wild and reading about it. An idea started to form, gaining traction and growing until it took up my entire mind. My anger ebbed away, replaced by steely determination. I was going to run away.

I thumped down the stairs. Our floorboards creaked. I raced out the door, not caring if my parents heard me, and pulled my bike from its rack, the scraping sound screeching like an angry animal. Mounting my bike, I turned my head and hollered at the top of my lungs: "I'm leaving and you can't stop me."

Then I pushed off and hurtled down the street, dirt and pebbles skittering out of my way like frightened people. A shout of anger could be heard, most certainly from my dad. And as I peddled away, I looked back. I got farther and farther away, and I saw the figure of my dad, seemingly yelling at me. I smiled. I had made my parents angry, and this time, they couldn't punish me.

After endless peddling, I sat on a rock near my new camp. I was free. I felt as if the tight bonds that had been restraining me all my life had broken. Finally, I could do whatever I wanted to do; no one could stop me. I looked up. The sky was a warm russet, stained with pink, blue, and purple.

Tears (Watercolor, acrylic)
Saira Merchant, 12
Bellaire, TX

A light shone through the woods. My heart jumped into my throat.
*Was that a mass murderer, shining a light through the woods,
looking for me?*

But what caught my attention were the birds that flew toward the scarlet sun. They dove and spiraled through the endless open air, getting further and further away, as if they loved the wind on their wings.

Night began to fall, and the light faded away. I found myself suffocating in the darkness around me, and even worse, strange sounds started to cut through the quiet—crackling and snapping, and squelches and thumps. They sent shivers down my neck. Mosquitoes gathered around me. I shook out my can of bug spray, only to find that it didn't work.

"It will work," I muttered, panic creeping into my voice. "I haven't messed up . . ."

I pressed over and over. Nothing. The buzzing of the bugs around me sounded like the jeering of my parents. I hated this stupid can. I flung it to the ground, the clatter of metal against rock jolting me. I dashed into the cave, flinging myself into my sleeping bag. This was all wrong. I was supposed to have a good night. I was supposed to be victorious. I lay there for a few minutes, the disappointment engulfing me thoroughly.

It began to get cold, too. Really cold. I shivered. My sleeping bag felt threadbare. Chills racked my body in fits of shaking. The bugs were still there, but the cold outweighed them by so much. I rolled around restlessly, and soon the bottom of my sleeping bag was drenched in dew. It felt like ice under my body. My teeth couldn't stop chattering as I forced myself out of bed. I pulled a lollipop from my backpack and tried to take off the wrapper. The lollipop seemed to be stuck to it. I was determined to make something go right, so I pulled once more. Finally, the wrapper came free. The candy was melted and sticky, all over the place, and flecks had clung to my hand, and now it was stuck to the stick. Tears stung my eyes as I looked at another failure.

Suddenly, a car screeched somewhere nearby. The door opened; footsteps rang out. I dropped my lollipop. It fell to the ground. A light shone through the woods. My heart jumped into my throat. *Was that a mass murderer, shining a light through the woods, looking for me?*

Then a voice sounded from the darkness. It was shaky, high, and familiar. It was the voice that had scolded me, chided me, and known me for ten long years. Mom and Dad. A million thoughts raced inside my head. *Should I call out to them?* But at the same time, I felt so satisfied that they were worried. It was clear from Mom's quivering voice, and the trembling beam of light, that they were worried. I moved forward, trying to get a closer look, but then I stumbled, scraping my knee hard on the ground. When I managed to get up again, no voice or light could be seen or heard. My parents were gone.

I curled up in the sleeping bag.

The bug bites on my face, neck, arms, and legs itched furiously, and I rolled around trying to scratch them. The freezing wind stung my face, and there was a numb cold all throughout my body. The place where I had scraped my knee burned with raw pain. I could feel blood leaking from the wound. My stomach was a churning hole. I would have thrown up, but I had eaten almost nothing since lunch. My throat was dry, begging for water, but all of my water was gone. I had drunk it when I'd arrived. My muscles ached. I scrunched into a ball, tears falling softly from my cheeks. I wanted to go home.

I don't know how long I lay there. I kept seeing my bedroom, where I could have been had I not run away. At the same time, I remembered the feeling of awe and happiness I had felt during sunset. I tried to hold onto it, but I couldn't. Slowly, it started to shrink, until it was only a speck in my memory. *Had I really been so happy, when I was so despaired now?* It didn't seem possible. I realized something then, with the mist of early morning dampening my battered, bruised, and bug-bitten face: I couldn't survive like this. I had to go home.

I mounted my bike, starting to pedal up the road. I felt as if I might combust at any moment, not just because of my weariness and my battered state, but also because of the emotions—anger, pain, despair—that were fighting inside of me.

As I rode, I thought maybe I hadn't been the best during the times my parents punished me. *Maybe . . . No.* I couldn't believe what I was thinking.

My parents had been wrong. But still, maybe running away hadn't been the best approach to my problems.

I looked up. I saw a house up ahead. It looked so familiar. I seemed to remember picking flowers with Mom in this very backyard. I thought I could recall sitting with Dad on the porch swing while he told me a story. These happy memories seemed so long ago, part of a different life, yet so close, full of warmth that was in my heart now. I felt as if our family was slowly mending, as if our bonds, the bonds that had withered in the past years, were regrowing.

The lights were on in all the downstairs windows, and figures could be seen pacing inside. Mom and Dad. Excitement and fear battled inside me. I wasn't sure whether to laugh and wave my arms, or hide, or stomp in and demand a lawyer. But then the two figures stopped and looked out the window.

I couldn't help it. I unlocked the door and flung myself into my parents' arms. Tears, this time of joy, poured down my face. I was home again!

Untitled (iPhone SE)
Octavius Doherty, 13
Pittsburgh, PA

My Fourth of July Surprise

A family celebrates the Fourth of July

By Melia Zhou, 8
Wilmette, IL

It was the Fourth of July, and my family and I were just finishing eating dinner outside on our patio. A few seconds after we finished, a crackling sound came behind us. We saw a glow of light and heard a loud clap; right after, a bunch of sparks came flying out of the light and started to fade. We watched the fireworks for fifteen minutes, and I asked my dad if we could start a fire in the fireplace and use our sparklers. He said yes to me. After the fire was going, my dad went to the garage to get the sparklers. Right when we lit them, four bright fireworks came into view. All of a sudden, rain came falling down so hard it sounded like someone was beating a drum. The rain got heavier and the fire was put out. We all ran home as fast as we could. Inside was cozy and warm. And we all decided to go to sleep.

America the Beautiful (Fujifilm XP)
Astrid Young, 12
Brookline, MA

Kleptocracy

By Trevor M. Burns, 10
Tucson, AZ

Kleptocracy is not Democracy
It is a word that's not heard
But should be without a single word
of a bird high in the sky
who would not die

Highlight from Stonesoup.com

From the Stone Soup Blog

Goodbye to "Happily Ever After": A Review of *Little Women*

By Grace Huang, 13
Skillman, NJ

Kind Cinderella lives luxuriously in a castle after enduring her hardships obediently. Gentle Snow White gets saved by the dashing prince because of her sweet personality. Loving Sleeping Beauty wakes up from her slumber with a single kiss. Characters in these cherished fairy tales we've grown up with always end up with their dreams being fulfilled—if they've been virtuous. Then what explains what happens to the girls in *Little Women* by Louisa May Alcott?

Little Women documents the growth of four very different sisters—Meg, Jo, Beth, and Amy—from childhood to womanhood. Each sister symbolizes a distinct type of personality, but how they end up in life doesn't match readers' initial expectations. By steering us away from our preconceptions, Alcott accurately depicts what life is really like: sometimes unfair and cruel, yet undeniably satisfying. From Alcott, I learned to accept that "happily ever after" doesn't exist, nor is it ultimately gratifying.

My mom had recommended this book to me, but I was hesitant to read it because the story of four girls didn't initially intrigue me. However, after learning that Alcott's father, Amos Bronson Alcott, was a friend of Emerson's and a leader in the transcendentalist movement of the time, I decided to try it. How might Alcott's feminine perspective of this period add to my understanding? I soon became lost in the intriguing plot, which takes place during the Civil War, and realized that this novel offers so much more than I had anticipated. The hardship the characters had to endure during this difficult period in American life and the complex moral message for women of all ages have had a lasting impact on me.

Though they grew up in the same household, the sisters are all quite different, and each is sharply drawn. Meg dreams of ending up in the lap of luxury but is eventually content with something quite the opposite. Jo, a classic tomboy, learns to balance her literary ambitions with tenderness. Beth, an ever-dutiful daughter, willingly resides at her cozy home without any further aspirations, while Amy grows from a pampered little girl to an ardent artist.

My two favorite characters are Jo and Amy, despite the fact that they are opposites. Both are ambitious girls, but Amy's graceful manners are what society valued in a woman at the time, while Jo's headstrong spirit is often questioned. Even though frivolous Amy almost always winds up better off than Jo, Alcott twists our expectations to ensure that each girl ends up content in her own way. It's a harsh truth that practicality sometimes wins out over idealism and that being virtuous doesn't ensure a happy ending.

You can read the rest of Grace's review on our website.

About the Stone Soup Blog

We publish original work—writing, art, book reviews, multimedia projects, and more—by young people on the Stone Soup Blog. You can read more posts by young bloggers, and find out more about submitting a blog post, here: https://stonesoup.com/stone-soup-blog/.

Honor Roll

Welcome to the Stone Soup Honor Roll. Every month, we receive submissions from hundreds of kids from around the world. Unfortunately, we don't have space to publish all the great work we receive. We want to commend some of these talented writers and artists and encourage them to keep creating.

STORIES

Nishka Budalakoti, 10
Miya Lin, 10

ART

Prisha Gandhi, 7
Angelica Gary, 11
Nari Woo Park, 10

MEMOIR

Jordana Blumenthal, 12
Riley Brown, 11
Esperanza Santelices, 12
Mattea Spivey, 10
Xuyi (Lauren) Zheng, 11

POETRY

Catherine Wright, 9

CPSIA information can be obtained
at www.ICGtesting.com
Printed in the USA
BVHW091931060622
638846BV00001B/1